Horace

ON THE ART OF POETRY

〔古罗马〕贺拉斯 著

诗 艺

王厚平 王洁 导读 注释

上海译文出版社

WAC

World Academic Classics

世界学术经典·英文版

总策划／总主编

庄智象　林骧华

上海时代教育出版研究中心 研发

Shanghai Epoch Education Publishing Research Center

世界学术经典（英文版）

总　序

书之成为经典，乃人类在不同时代的思想、智慧与学术的结晶，优秀文化之积淀，具有不随时代变易的永恒价值。有道是读书须读经典，这是智者的共识。

对于中外经典著作中的思想表述，仅读外文书的中译本或文言著作的白话释文是不够的，尤其是当误译、误释发生的时候，读者容易被误导，或望文生义，或以讹传讹，使原有的文化差异变成更深的文化隔阂。因此，在“世界学术经典（英文版）”的选目中，大部分作品为英文原著；原作是其他语种的经典，则选用相对可靠的英文译本；至于中国古代经典，则采用汉英对照的方式呈现，旨在向西方阐释中国的思想和文化。其中，精选的中国经典是整个系列的重要组成部分。有了这一部分的经典，才真正体现出“世界性”。

以原典和英文方式出版，是为了使读者通过研读，准确理解以英文表达的思想、理论和方法，力求避免舛误，进而通过批判和接受，化为智慧力量。这有利于思想的传播，裨益于新思想的产生，同时亦可提高英语修养。

经典名著的重要性是不言而喻的，但是以下几点意义值得一再重申。

（一）学术经典提供思想源泉

两千六百年来的世界学术经典凝聚了人类思想的精华，

世世代代的优秀思想家以他们独特的见识和智慧，留给后人取之不竭、用之不尽的思想源泉。从老子、孔子、柏拉图、亚里士多德以降，天才辈出，思想闪光，精彩纷呈。思想界的大师、名家们在人类思想史传统链条上的每一个环节，都启发后人开拓新的思想领域，探究生命的本质，直抵人性的深层。随着人类思想的不断成熟和完善，各个学科领域的理论从本体论、认识论、方法论、实践论、价值论等维度不断深化。后人继承前人的思想，借经典的滋养保持思想活力，丰富和发展前人的观点，使之形成一波又一波的思想洪流，从而改变人的思想和世界观，改变人类社会的进程。历史已经证明：人类社会的进步，思想的力量大于一切。

（二）学术经典传承精神力量

经典名著中蕴含的人类精神，传承的人类守望的共同价值原则和社会理想，在每一个具体领域里都有诸多丰富的表述，它们从整体上构成了推动人类进步的精神力量。研习和传承人类两千六百多年来的优秀思想，并将它化作求新求变的灵感，是人类文明的要义所在。仅有技术进步，还不足以表明人类的文明程度。若无优秀的思想底蕴，人类存在的意义将大打折扣。

中国思想传统中的基本理念和西方思想传统中的基本理念分别形成了东西方两大具有普遍价值的道德观念和价值系统。值得注意的是：(1) 这两大道德系统应该是一个互补、互鉴的整体，两者都不可偏废，因为人类的思想是个多元整体。任何一个民族，缺少其中之一，在精神上都可能是不完整的；(2) 这些基本理念都不是抽象概念，它们都具有很强的实践意义，并且必须由实践来考察，否则就很难体现其价值。

精神传承必然是一种自觉的过程，它靠习得，不靠遗传，因此我们需要研读经典。

（三）学术经典构成文化积淀

“文化”包含三大部分：(1) 思想与精神现象；(2) 制度与习俗；(3) 有形的事物。学术经典是对思想与精神现象的归纳和提炼，对制度与习俗的探究和设计，对有形事物的形而上思考和描述。

每一个学科领域的经典著作中都会提出一些根本性的

问题，这些问题直面人的困惑，思考人类社会的疑难，在新思想和新知识中展现人类的智慧。当这些思想成果积淀下来，就构成人类文化的主要组成部分。文化不只是制度或器物的外在形式，更重要的是凝结在其背后的精神与思想。

每一个学科的学术本身都要面对一些形而上的（超越性的、纯理论性的）文化问题。在很多人看来，理性的思考和理论的表述都是很枯燥的，但是热爱真理并且对思想情有独钟的人会从学术经典的理论中发现无限生动的天地，从而产生获得真理的快乐，这才是我们追求的真正文化。

大量阅读经典名著是一种学习、积累文化的根本方法，深度阅读和深刻记忆能使文化积淀在人的身上，并且代代相传。假如这一过程中断了，人世间只剩下花天酒地、歌舞升平，文化也就湮灭了。

（四）学术经典推动社会进步

毫无疑问，凡属学术经典，都必须含有新的学术成果——新思想、新理论、新方法，或者新探索。这样的原创性学术成果越多，人类的思想就越深邃，视野越开阔，理论更全面、完美，方法更先进、有效，社会的进步才能获得新的动力和保障。

人文主义推翻神学，理性主义旨在纠正人的偏激，启蒙精神主张打破思想束缚，多元主义反抗绝对理念。各种新思想层出不穷，带来了学术的进步，启发并推动了更大的社会变革。这些原创思想在历史长河中经过漫长的时间考验，成为经典，在任何一种文明中都是社会进步和发展的动力。

当我们研读完一部学术经典，分析和归纳其原创的思想观点时，可以很清晰地理解和感悟它在同时代的环境里对于社会的变革和进步有着何种意义，以及它对当下有哪些启迪。

相比技术的发展，思想并不浮显在社会的表层，它呈现在书本的字里行间，渗透于人的心智，在人的灵魂中闪光。每当社会需要时，它能让我们看到无形的巨大力量。

温故而知新。今日世界纷乱依旧，但时代已不再朦胧。人类思想史上的各种主张，在实践中都已呈现清晰的面貌。当我们重新梳理各种思想和理论时，自然不会再返回到“全盘接受”或者“全盘否定”的幼稚阶段。二十一世纪人类正确的世界观、人生观、价值观需要优秀思想传统的支撑，并通过批判继承，不断推陈出新，滋衍出磅礴之推力。

我们所选的这些学术经典，成书于不同的时代，代表了不同的思想与理论主张。有些著作带有时代烙印，有其局限性或片面性；有些观点不一定正确，但从另一个方面显示出人类思想的丰富性和复杂性。各门学科建立、各种主张提出之后，都曾经在历代思想的实验场上经受碰撞和检验，被接受或者被批判。我们的学者需要研读这些书，而青年学生们的思想成长更需要读这些书。当然，批评与分析是最有效和最有益的阅读方法。

有鉴于此，我们希望“世界学术经典（英文版）”能够真正做到“开卷有益”，使我们自己在潜移默化中都成长为有思想、有理想、有品位的人。

上海时代教育出版研究中心

2018 年 10 月

目 录

导　读

王厚平　王　洁

贺拉斯全名昆图斯·贺拉斯·弗拉库斯（Quintus Horatius Flaccus，公元前65—前8），是古罗马帝国奥古斯都统治时期著名的诗人、批评家、翻译家，生逢古罗马文学的“黄金时代”，与维吉尔（Virgil，公元前70—前19）、奥维德(Ovid，公元前43—17)并称为古罗马三大诗人。贺拉斯出生于意大利韦诺萨（Venosa）边界地带的贸易重镇，这里由于人口混杂，日常交流和贸易往来的各种语言交织在一起，在一定程度上丰富了他的语感，也是由于这个原因，有学者推测贺拉斯在很小的时候就已经接触到了希腊语——这一他从中汲取了艺术和思想精华的语言。贺拉斯的父亲曾经做奴隶，幸而在儿子出生前就获得了自由，并成为一名拍卖师的助手，才得以教养贺拉斯。他很看重对贺拉斯的启蒙，在贺拉斯年纪尚小时陪他去罗马最好的学府接受教育，贺拉斯对父亲也十分敬重，在《讽刺集》（Satirae）的献词中曾表达对父亲的感激之情，认为自己的父亲配得上世界上最热烈的称颂之词。父亲去世后，贺拉斯离开罗马，去往当时的学术中心雅典求学，19 岁时进入到柏拉图建立的学园，也正是在这个时候，他开始慢慢了解古希腊抒情诗的价值所在。

贺拉斯著有抒情诗一卷、讽刺诗两卷、颂歌四卷、书信集两卷。12 世纪的一位学者对他的作品进行了总结："贺拉斯以四个年龄写了四种不同的诗歌，写给男孩的《颂歌》、年轻人的《诗艺》、成熟男士的《讽刺集》以及暮年的《书信集》。"古罗马修辞学家、演说家昆体良（Quintilian，约35—约95）认为贺拉斯的颂歌（odes）是唯一值得反复吟咏的拉丁文颂歌，称赞他笔下塑造的人物形象饱满，并且在选词方面大胆创新，不落窠臼。除了作品，昆体良对贺拉斯本人的评价也很高，认为他有时或许有点高傲，但其人仪态优雅，充满魅力。

贺拉斯的职业生涯恰逢罗马从共和国到帝国的重大转变，当时他结识了屋大维的助手，并成为新政体的发言人，有些评论家认为他自主判断能力很强，与新政权之间达到了一种微妙的平衡。不仅如此，贺拉斯在当时的学术界也有盛名，常有人向他请教知识，《诗艺》就是于公元前19年写给罗马贵族皮索父子三人的诗体信简，用六音步诗行进行创作，全诗共四百七十六行。信中总结了罗马的文学现状，并对文学创作提出了自己的意见。原名是《答皮索父子书》(Epistula ad Pisones)，经过一个世纪，昆体良在他的著作《雄辩术原理》(Institutio Oratoria）中将其取名为《诗艺》(Ars Poetica)。朱光潜先生在《西方美学史》里评论《诗艺》对于西方文艺影响之大时，认为其仅次于亚里士多德的《诗学》，有时在某些方面甚至还超过了它。

《诗艺》大致上可分为三个部分，主要讲述诗的艺术形式、创作方法以及诗人个人天赋和后天实践的重要性。因为这是一封带有诗意色彩的书信，是为欣赏诗歌文学的朋友们撰写的，所以每个部分之间的内在逻辑并不是很讲究，有时从一个主题到另一个主题的过渡有些突兀，主题的排列也比较随意，然而漫不经心只是表象，真知灼见却在其中。贺拉斯在《诗艺》中提及当时罗马的文学创作现状时就曾指出，有些作家追求平淡，但是却缺失了魄力，没有价值；有些作家为了追求所谓崇高而选用浮夸之词，贺拉斯将这种文章称之为“purpureus pannus”，字面意思是“紫色补丁”，华丽而无用。那些描述太过夸张或者华丽的散文句子、段落，有时甚至是整篇文学作品都有可能属于这类缺陷；而有些作家一味追求标新立异，写出来的东西却不合常理，就如在森林里画海豚、海浪里画野猪一样，不伦不类，弄巧反拙。

针对出现的这些问题，贺拉斯提出了自己的见地——“合式”（decorum）原则的运用。按照贺拉斯的观点，诗所具备的品质就是“合式”。《诗艺》开篇便举了一个例子来说明“合式”原则，假设一幅画上的人物，人头接马颈，四肢是由各种动物的肢体拼凑，覆盖着各色羽毛，下面长着一条又黑又丑的鱼尾巴，这种画作匪夷所思，何来美感？“合式”原则是贺拉斯为艺术创作从内容到形式确立的具体标准，主要指体裁、人物性格、故事情节、语言风格的恰当得体，需要符合自然法则以及观众心理，目的是为了寻求诗歌的统一与完美。贺拉斯在《诗艺》中针对“合式”原则，提到不同的体裁要采用不同的词句，例如：喜剧主题就不能使用悲剧的诗句，不同的角色，年龄、身份地位以及所处的社会背景有别，气质和谈吐自然也会不同，什么样的角色说什么样的话，不要把儿童或者青年写成老人的性格。尤其是一些经典史诗中的人物，他们的性格早已深入人心，是不能够轻易更改的，这一观点在亚里士多德《诗学》第十四章也有体现。但是与亚里士多德不同的是，贺拉斯鼓励在选择题材以及塑造人物性格上大胆创新，不过，他也在文中提醒作者，如果敢于塑造一个新人物，那么就必须要注意人物性格需要从头到尾保持一致，不可自相矛盾。按照“合式”原则，贺拉斯对戏剧也作出了一系列要求，如一部戏剧应该恰好有五幕，台上最多有三个演员说话，这些指导性原则成为日后古典主义的信条。

贺拉斯认为文艺应该摹仿古典，特别是古希腊的艺术杰作，他在《诗艺》中对古希腊的古典作品极度推崇，建议皮索父子三人“你们需学习希腊古典作品，日夜不辍”，这句话日后成为法国新古典主义运动中的响亮口号和鲜明旗帜。贺拉斯为何如此推崇古希腊文化？这与当时罗马的社会背景息息相关，西方文学在古希腊时期已经达到了自己的第一个高峰，但是罗马不断扩张，人口数量快速增长。亚历山大去世后，西方的政治中心逐渐从希腊转到了罗马，古希腊文化逐渐衰落。但罗马当时的文艺创造却远不如军事和政治那样可以夸耀世界。随着工商业的发展，罗马在公元前1世纪到达了鼎盛时期，即奥古斯都时代。繁荣的背后也存在不少问题，生产力的发展与落后的奴隶生产之间的矛盾日益突出，为了维持政权，统治者将精力投入到一些能使国力更加强盛的领域，尤其是在军事、交通、农业、法律等与综合国力相关的方面下了很大功夫，却没有心思在文艺上花费过多精力，使得当时罗马的文学创作几为空白。不过，因为希腊与罗马在意识形态上基本一致，都是奴隶主社会，所以罗马就自然地接受了伟大的希腊古典文化，以致当时的罗马人有“征服者被征服”的感叹。贺拉斯生逢这个时代，极力宣扬罗马的文艺创作应当向古希腊学习，如选材需要遵循传统，古典作品中的人物性格应该与之前作品的描写相一致，格律也主张采用希腊诗的格律。他的这些文艺创作主张，目的是要在继承希腊传统的基础上，使罗马作家能够创作出属于自己民族和时代的新篇章，让罗马的文艺成就能够与古希腊的典范相媲美。

《诗艺》中提到："我们的诗人尝试过各种类型的戏剧，他们不落于希腊人的窠臼，并且以本国的题材写成悲剧或喜剧"。贺拉斯鼓励诗人创作新词和新人物，称新词是带有时代烙印的词，像青春的年华，繁荣昌盛。他认为大家都有这种自由权，一个新造词也有可能流行于世，为语言注入新鲜血液，因为人类语言的朽灭更替符合语言变化的规律，他所主张的这种创作方式是古罗马文学得以重生的主要因素。

关于诗的功用问题，贺拉斯认为诗有"寓教于乐"的功能，在诗中能够使娱乐和教益相结合，这一点也是诗人的职责所在。在《诗艺》中，贺拉斯明确强调了诗的这两大功能，诗不仅能够教化人类放弃野蛮的生活，建立城市的秩序，还能鼓舞人心，传达神谕，指示人生道路。在教诲别人时，话要说的言简意赅，容易让人接受，既能给予读者快感，又能让他们品格得到提升，这样的作品才能成为经典。这样的理论似乎就成为了一个公式，为文艺复兴和新古典主义时代的文艺理论奠定了基础，从文艺复兴时代起，欧洲不断地出现所谓的“诗的辩护”，大体都是摹仿《诗艺》中的口吻。“寓教于乐说”揭示了文艺的道德教化功用和审美娱乐功用的互补关系。

除了论述诗人承担的教化职责之外，《诗艺》中对诗人之所以为诗人，也作出了一定的要求。

贺拉斯认为，一切佳作的源泉无不在于诗人个人的思想修养，因此不能让金钱和贪婪的欲望腐蚀了人的心灵。还有，如果碰到一些“疯狂的”诗人，最好敬而远之，因为你不知道他内心在想些什么，也要避免成为这样的人。在这一点上，柏拉图与贺拉斯的观点正好相反，柏拉图认为，诗人只有在丧失理智，进入迷狂状态时才会有灵感，才有能力进行创作。表面上看来是两种观点的对立，实际上是理智在艺术中的作用问题，柏拉图认为理智在文艺的创作上用处不大，所以片面地否定了理智的作用；而贺拉斯作为古典主义者，重视理性和节制，这些因素自然也会反映其在文艺创作理论的方方面面。

其次在选材时，他主张诗人要选择自己能够胜任的题材。这里贺拉斯是在批评写大型史诗的诗人，这些诗人把特洛伊战争从头写到尾，事无巨细，全都囊括在内，但是大而无当，力不从心。不如像荷马那样，以特洛伊战争中的一件小事为主线，将其他事件穿插进去，结构和逻辑上都很清晰，能有始有终地完成作品。至于是遵循传统题材来创作，还是独创题材，他虽认为两者均可，但更倾向于“遵循传统”，即沿用传统题材比较容易一些，也比较容易为人所接受。已经知道自己要写什么的作家，则需要到生活中去寻找灵感。艺术来源于生活，一出戏剧由于人物形象刻画恰当，即使没有华丽的辞藻或者技巧，也能获得观众的喜爱。在这之中，尤其要注意戏剧情节的真实性。情节可以在舞台上展示，也可以通过演员来叙述。虽然前者打动人心灵的程度要比后者高，但是不该在舞台上演出的就不要表演出来，例如美狄亚杀子、复仇的阿特柔斯煮人肉、普洛克涅变幻成鸟以及请神来搭救，即使虚构也要贴近现实，否则，演出来只会让观众质疑情节的真实性，甚至会产生游离于情节之外的怪诞感受。《诗艺》中还提到天资与后天习得之间的关系，苦学而无天资或是有天资而不苦学都毫无用处，两者必须结合起来，才能成功，这一观点在朗吉努斯的《论崇高》中也曾提及。

从上述观点中我们可以看出，贺拉斯对于诗人的要求已经显示出强调诗人自我表现的重要，他认为一首诗仅仅具有美是不够的，还必须要有魅力；你自己要先笑，别人才会笑；自己要先哭，才能引得别人哭。这里强调的魅力就是打动人的情感力量，也就是美感的力量。这种力量源自诗人的内在修养和表现力。

贺拉斯在《诗艺》中也谈及文艺评判的标准问题，他建议皮索父子找一些批评家来评论自己的作品，不要怕批评，因为只有指出问题，才能改进，才能有所进步。如果知道自己的作品有问题却执意不改，这样才会贻笑大方。但是需要注意一些阿谀奉承的人，如果一个诗人很富有，必定会招来很多牟利之徒；让这些人来评判他的诗，他们必定会高声赞叹，这样得出的评价并不客观，这也是对当时罗马文坛上不良风气的批判。对于诗歌中可能出现的错误，贺拉斯认为是瑕不掩瑜，如果一首诗的优点很多，即使有点小缺陷，也遮不住光辉，但是如果多次犯同样的错误，那就不可原谅了。他关于作品评判的另一个观点就是赏诗就如赏画一般，有的需要放在眼前，有的需要放在远处，好的作品就不怕时代的考验，认为文艺作品如果能经得起各阶层读者在长时期里的考验，持久行远，才能算得上真正好的作品或者经典。

《诗艺》作为文学艺术理论经典著作之一，在欧洲古代文艺创作中起着承上启下的作用：上承亚里士多德的《诗学》，下启文艺复兴时期文艺理论和古典文艺理论之端，对17世纪和18世纪的古典主义思想起了极大的推动作用。贺拉斯的古典主义思想在《诗艺》中表现得淋漓尽致，他将自己所理解的古典作品中最好的品质和经验教训总结出来，对文艺现象做出全面而合理的认识，提出了独有创新的见解：既要从生活中获取创作灵感，又要大胆地运用想象；

既要遵循古典文艺的形式与技巧，又要力求创新，为自己所用；既要重视文艺的道德教化作用，又要从中获得快乐。贺拉斯是西方文论史上第一位明确地注意到受众的心理反映的人，因为他意识到了文艺本身作为一种传播媒介应该具有的接受反映美感。《诗艺》中提出的文艺评价的标准对欧美戏剧的发展亦影响深远，对诗人所应具备的素养，提出的相关要求在当今也有很强的指导意义。《诗艺》虽是一篇文艺批评短简，却是古罗马诗人贺拉斯富有灵感的艺术创作和审美体验的总结，可谓字字珠玑，对于今天的文艺创作和美学研究仍有学习和借鉴价值。

HORACE

On the Art of Poetry

HORACE On the Art of Poetry

SUPPOSING a painter chose to put a human head on a horse's neck, or to spread feathers of various colours over the limbs of several different creatures, or to make what in the upper part is a beautiful woman tail off into a hideous[1] fish, could you help laughing when he showed

1. hideous: 丑陋的

you his efforts? You may take it from me, my friends[1], that a book will have very much the same effect as these pictures if, like a sick man's dreams, the author's idle fancies assume such a shape that it is impossible to make head or tail of what he is driving at. 'But,' you will say, 'the right to take liberties of almost any kind has always been enjoyed by painters and poets alike.' I know that; we poets do claim this licence, and in our turn we concede[2] it to others, but not to the point of associating what is wild with what is tame, of pairing snakes with birds or lambs with tigers.

---

1. my friends：这里称呼的是古罗马贵族皮索父子，《诗艺》是作者写给他们的信简。
2. concede：给予

Works that begin impressively and with the promise of carrying on in the heroic strain often have one or two purple passage[1] tacked on to catch the eye, giving a description of Diana's grove[2] and altar, the meanderings of a stream through a picturesque countryside, the River Rhine, or a rainbow. But this is not the right place for things of that kind. Perhaps, too, you know how to paint a cypress[3]; but what is the point of that if you are being paid to paint a shipwrecked man swimming for dear life? A potter sets out to make

1. purple passage：辞藻过于华丽的文本。贺拉斯自创，指描述太过夸张或华丽的文句、段落，有时甚至是整篇作品。
2. grove：树林；林地，此处指古罗马神话中月亮和狩猎女神黛安娜的林地。
3. cypress：柏树

a two-handled wine-flagon: why, as his wheel spins, does it turn into an ordinary water-jug? In short, whatever you set your hand to, you must be single-minded about it and keep to the point.

Most of us poets, my friends, are led astray by our notions of the right way to go to work. I try my hardest to be succinct[1], and merely succeed in being obscure; I aim at smoothness, only to find that I am losing fire and energy. One poet sets out to achieve the sublime, and falls into turgidity[2]; another is over-cautious, and, nervous of spreading his wings, never leaves the ground. Yet another, wishing to vary the monotony

---

1. succinct：简明的；言简意赅的
2. turgidity：浮夸

of his subject with something out of the ordinary, introduces a dolphin into his woods, or puts a boar[1] among his waves. If art is lacking, the avoidance of a petty fault may lead to a serious imperfection.

At the end of the row of stalls down by the Aemilian gladiatorial school[2] there is a craftsman in bronze who will mould fingernails and reproduce wavy hair to the life, but the total effect of his work is unsatisfactory because he cannot put together a complete figure. Now if I set out to write a poem, I would no more want to be like him than to have a crooked nose, much though

1. boar：野猪
2. the Aemilian gladiatorial school：埃米里乌斯角斗士学校，由执政官埃米里乌斯在古罗马建立。

I might be admired for my dark eyes and black hair.

Choose a subject that is suited to your abilities, you who aspire to be writers; give long thought to what you are capable of undertaking, and what is beyond you. A man who chooses a subject within his powers will never be at a loss for words, and his thoughts will be clear and orderly. The virtue and attraction of order, I think I am right in saying, is that the poet will at any moment be saying exactly what his poem at that moment requires; he will be keeping back points for the time being or leaving them out altogether, and showing what he thinks admirable and what beneath notice.

Furthermore, you will make an excellent impression

if you use care and subtlety in placing your words and, by the skilful choice of setting, give fresh meaning to a familiar word. If it happens that you have to invent new terms for the discussion of abstruse[1] topics, you will have a chance to coin words that were unknown to earlier generations of Romans, and no one will object to your doing this, as long as you do it with discretion[2]. New and recently-coined words will win acceptance if they are borrowed from Greek sources and drawn upon sparingly[3]. And indeed, why should we Romans

---

1. abstruse：深奥的
2. discretion：谨慎；审慎的态度
3. sparingly：适量地

allow this privilege to Caecilius[1] and Plautus[2], and refuse it to Virgil[3] and Varius[4]? Why should I be grudged the right to add a few words to the stock if I can, when the language of Cato[5] and Ennius[6] has enriched our native speech by the introduction of new terms? It has always been accepted, and always will be, that words stamped with the mintmark of the day[7] should be brought into currency. As the woods

1. Caecilius：凯齐留斯，古罗马修辞学者。
2. Plautus：普劳图斯（公元前 254？—前 184），古罗马喜剧作家。
3. Virgil：维吉尔（公元前 70—前 19），古罗马的伟大诗人。
4. Varius：瓦里乌斯（公元前 74—前 14），贺拉斯同时代诗人。
5. Cato：加图（公元前 234—前 149），古罗马政治家、演说家，是古罗马时期第一位重要的拉丁语散文作家。
6. Ennius：恩尼乌斯（公元前 239—前 169），古罗马诗人。
7. mintmark of the day：时代的标志；时代印记

change their foliage with the decline of each year, and the earliest leaves fall, so words die out with old age; and the newly born ones thrive and prosper just like human beings in the vigour of youth. We are all destined to die, we and all our works. Perhaps the land has been dug out and an arm of the sea let in, to give protection to our fleets from the northern gales[1] (and what a royal undertaking this was!); a or a marsh[2], long a barren waste on which oars were plied, has been put under the plough and produces food for the neigh-bouring towns; or a river has been made to change a course ruinous to the cornfields and turned

---

1. gales：飓风；大风
2. marsh：湿地；沼泽

into a straighter channel: whatever they are, the works of men will pass away. How much less likely are the glory and grace of language to have an enduring life! Many terms that have now dropped out of use will be revived, if usage so requires, and others which are now in repute will die out; for it is usage which regulates the laws and conventions of speech.

Homer showed us in what metre[1] the exploits of kings and commanders and the miseries of war were to be recorded. The elegiac couplet[2] was first used as the vehicle for lament, but was later adopted for

---

1. metre：格律
2. elegiac couplet：挽歌对句。通常首行六个音步，次行五个音步，最初见于挽歌，后用于赞美诗。

verses of thanksgiving; however, scholars argue about who devised this slighter elegiac form, and the case so far rests undecided. Archilochus[1] invented the iambic measure as the weapon for furious satire; it was adopted both for comedy and for high tragedy, since it is appropriate for dialogue, is capable of drowning the noises of the audience, and is by its nature well suited to accompany action. To lyrical poetry the Muse assigned the task of celebrating the gods and their offspring, the winner in a boxing-match, and the horse that led the field; the task, too, of singing the woes of young lovers and the pleasures of wine. If I have not

---

1. Archilochus：阿尔基罗库斯（公元前680—前645），古希腊抒情诗人。

the ability and skill to adhere to these well-defined functions and styles of poetic forms, why should I be hailed as a poet? Why out of false shame should I prefer to remain ignorant rather than to learn my craft? A comic subject is not susceptible of treatment in a tragic style, and similarly the banquet of Thyestes[1] cannot be fitly described in the strains of everyday life or in those that approach the tone of comedy. Let each of these styles be kept for the role properly allotted to it. Yet even comedy at times uses elevated language,

---

1. Thyestes：堤厄斯忒斯，古希腊神话中的人物，诱奸其嫂，其兄阿特柔斯（Atreus）为了报复，杀了堤厄斯忒斯的儿子并请其吃烹子宴，此种体裁为悲剧，不应用喜剧的日常谈吐。

and an angry Chremes[1] rails in bombastic terms; while in tragedy Telephus and Peleus[2] often express their grief in prosaic[3] language, and each of them in his poverty-stricken exile renounces his usual rant and his sesquipedalian[4] words when he wants to move the spectator's pity with his lamentation.

It is not enough that poems should have beauty; if they are to carry the audience with them, they must have charm as well. Just as smiling faces are turned on those who smile, so is sympathy shown with those

1. Chremes：克瑞墨斯，古罗马喜剧作家泰伦提乌斯作品中的人物，是个吝啬鬼。
2. Telephus and Peleus：特勒福斯和珀琉斯，两者都是古希腊悲剧中的人物。
3. prosaic：平淡的；散文体的
4. sesquipedalian：多音节的

who weep. If you want to move me to tears, you must first feel grief yourself; then, Telephus and Peleus, your misfortunes will grieve me too, whereas, if your speeches are out of harmony with your feelings, I shall either fall asleep or burst out laughing. Pathetic language is appropriate to the face of sorrow, and violent language to the face of anger; a sportive[1] diction goes with merry looks, and a serious with grave looks. For nature has so formed us that we first feel inwardly any change in our fortunes; it is she that cheers us or rouses us to anger, she that torments us and bows us to the ground with a heavy burden of sorrow, and it is

1. sportive：嬉戏的；欢闹的

only afterwards that she expresses these feelings in us by means of the tongue. If the speaker's words are out of key with his fortunes, a Roman audience will cackle[1] and jeer[2] to a man. It will make a great difference whether a god or a hero is speaking, a man of ripe years or a hot-headed youngster in the pride of youth, a woman of standing or an officious[3] nurse, a roving merchant or a prosperous farmer, a Colchian or an Assyrian, a man from Thebes or one from Argos.

Either follow the beaten track, or invent something that is consistent within itself. If in your play you

1. cackle：大笑
2. jeer：嘲笑；奚落人的话语
3. officious：爱管闲事的

happen to be representing the illustrious Achilles[1], let him be energetic, passionate, ruthless, and implacable; let him say that laws are not meant for him, and think that everything must yield to the force of arms. See to it that Medea[2] is fierce and indomitable, Ino[3] tearful, Ixion[4] faithless, Io a wanderer, and Orestes[5] sorrowful. If you introduce an untried subject to the stage, or are so bold as to invent a new character, be sure that it remains the same all the way through as it was at the beginning, and is entirely consistent.

---

1. Achilles：阿喀琉斯，古希腊神话中的英雄，特洛伊战争中表现神勇。
2. Medea：美狄亚，古希腊神话中的复仇女神。
3, 4, 5. Ino, Ixion, Orestes：伊诺、伊克西翁、俄瑞斯特斯，都是古希腊神话中的人物，贺拉斯在文中给出了这些人物的典型形象。

It is hard to be original in treating well-worn[1] subjects, and it is better for you to be putting a Trojan tale into dramatic form than that you should be first in the field with a theme hitherto unknown and unsung. A theme that is familiar can be made your own property as long as you do not waste your time on a hackneyed treatment; nor should you try to render your original word for word like a slavish translator, or in imitating another writer plunge yourself into difficulties from which shame, or the rules you have laid down for yourself, prevent you from extricating[2] yourself. And you must not, like the cyclic poet of old,

1. well-worn：老生常谈的
2. extricating：解救；使自己挣脱出来，这里动语用作名词。

begin: 'Of Priams'[1] fate I'll sing and war's renown.' What will emerge that can live up to such extravagant promises? The mountains will fall into labour, and there will be born — an absurd little mouse. How much more to the purpose are the words of the man[2] who makes no foolish undertakings: 'Sing for me, Muse, the man who, after the fall of Troy, made himself acquainted with the ways of many men and their cities.' This poet does not mean to let his flash of fire die away in smoke, but to make the smoke give way to light, when he may with striking effect relate

---

1. Priams：普里阿摩斯，古希腊神话中特洛伊的国王。
2. the man，上下文看，这里指的是《奥德赛》的作者荷马。

his tales of wonder, tales of Antiphates[1] and Scylla[2] and Charybdis[3] and the Cyclops[4]. He does not trace Diomede's return right back to the death of Meleager, or the Trojan War to the twin eggs of Leda. All the time he is hurrying on to the crisis, and he plunges his hearer into the middle of the story as if it were already familiar to him; and what he cannot hope to embellish by his treatment he leaves out. Moreover, so inventive is he, and so skilfully does he blend fact and fiction, that the middle is not inconsistent with the beginning, nor the end with the middle.

1, 2, 3, 4. Antiphates, Scylla, Charybdis, Cyclops：吃人妖怪安提法特斯、海妖斯库拉、漩涡怪卡律布狄斯、独眼巨人基克洛普斯，均为奥德赛在旅途中遭遇的艰难险阻。

I will tell you what I, and with me the public as a whole, look for in a play. If you want an appreciative hearer who will wait for the curtain and remain in his seat until the player calls out, 'Give us your applause', you must note the behaviour of people of different ages, and give the right kind of manners to characters of varying dispositions[1] and years. The child who has just learnt to speak and to plant his feet firmly on the ground loves playing with his friends, will fly into a temper and with as little reason recover from it, and will change every hour. The beardless youth who has at last got rid of his tutor finds his

1. dispositions：性情

pleasures in horses and dogs and the grassy sports-fields of the Campus Martius[1]; pliant as wax, he is easily persuaded to vicious courses, is irritable with his counsellors, slow to provide for his needs, lavish with his money, of high aspirations and passionate desires, and quick to abandon the objects of his fancy. When he is become a man in years and spirit, his inclinations change; he sets out to acquire wealth and influential connexions[2], aims at securing public offices, and is careful to avoid doing anything which he might later wish had been done otherwise. The old man is beset

---

1. the Campus Martius：战神广场（拉丁语意：玛尔斯的广场），名字取之于古罗马战神玛尔斯。
2. connexions：联系；纽带

by many troubles; either he tries to make money, but holds back miserably when it comes his way and is afraid to use it, or he is cautious and faint-hearted[1] in all his dealings; he puts things off, clings to his hopes, and remains inactive in an eager desire to prolong his life; he is obstinate, too, and querulous[2], and given to praising the days when he was a boy and criticizing and rebuking his juniors. Advancing years bring with them many blessings, but many of these are taken away in the decline of life. Thus, in order not to give a young man the characteristics of old age, or the child those of a grown man, we shall always dwell upon the

---

1. faint-hearted：胆小的
2. querulous：爱发牢骚的；爱抱怨的

qualities that are appropriate to a particular time of life.

An episode is either acted on the stage, or reported as having taken place. However, the mind is less actively stimulated by what it takes in through the ear than by what is presented to it through the trustworthy agency of the eyes — something that the spectator can see for himself. But you will not bring on to the stage anything that ought properly to be taking place behind the scenes, and you will keep out of sight many episodes that are to be described later by the eloquent tongue of a narrator. Medea must not butcher her children in the presence of the audience, nor the monstrous Atreus cook his dish of human flesh within public view, nor Procne[1] be metamorphosed into a bird, nor Cadmus[2] into a snake. I shall turn in disgust from anything of this kind that you show me.

If you want your play to be called for and given a second per-formance, it should not be either shorter or longer than five acts. A *deus ex machina*[3] should not be introduced unless some entanglement develops which requires such a person to unravel it. And there should not be more than three speaking characters on the stage at the same time.

---

1. Procne：普洛克涅，古希腊神话中雅典公主菲罗墨拉的姐姐，色雷斯王国之妻，后被神变成一只飞鸟。
2. Cadmus：卡德摩斯，古希腊神话中的人物，是忒拜城的建立者，后化为灵蛇。
3. *deus ex machina*：〈拉〉（古希腊罗马戏剧中用舞台机关送出来的）解围之神。

The Chorus should sustain the role and function of an actor, and should not sing anything between the acts that does not contribute to the plot and fit appropriately into it. It should side with the good characters and give them friendly advice, and should control those who are out of temper and show approval to those who are anxious not to transgress. It should commend moderation in the pleasures of the table, the blessings of law and justice, and times of peace when the gates lie open; it should respect confidences, and should pray and beseech[1] the gods to let prosperity return to the wretched and desert the proud.

---

1. beseech：祈求；恳求

At one time the flute — not as now bound with brass and a rival to the trumpet, but simple and delicate in tone and with only a few stops[1] — was of service in giving the note to the Chorus and accompanying it; and its soft music filled rows of seats that were not yet overcrowded, where an audience small enough to be counted came together — simple, thrifty folk, modest and virtuous in their ways. But when a conquering race began to extend its territories, and cities grew in size, and the tutelary[2] deity could be propitiated without fear of censure by drinking in the daytime on festal occasions, a greater freedom was allowed in the choice both of rhythms and

---

1. stops：（乐器的）孔
2. the tutelary：守护神

melodies. For what taste could be expected in a crowd of uneducated men enjoying a holiday from work, when country bumpkins rubbed shoulders with townsfolk, and slum-dwellers with men of rank? Thus the flute-player introduced wanton[1] movements that were unknown in the style of earlier days, and trailed his robe as he made his way over the stage. The grave lyre, too, acquired new notes, and a more abrupt type of eloquence brought with it a new style of speech in which wise saws and prophecies of the future caught the very manner of the Delphic oracle[2].

The poet originally competed in tragic verse for the

---

1. wanton：狂乱的；恣意的
2. the Delphic oracle：特尔斐神谕（常对问题作模棱两可的回答），作者在这里指台词难以理解。

paltry prize of a goat; soon he introduced wild and naked satyrs[1] on to the stage, and without loss of dignity tried his hand at a form of crude jesting; for an audience that was tipsy[2] after observing the Bacchic[3] rites and in a lawless mood could only be held by the attraction of some enticing novelty. But if jesters and mocking satyrs are to win approval, and a transition made from the serious to the light-hearted, it must be done in such a way that no one who has been presented as a god or hero, and who a moment ago was resplendent in purple and gold, is transported into a dingy hovel and

---

1. satyrs：古希腊神话中的森林之神萨梯，具人形而有羊的尾、耳、角等，此处比作好色之徒。
2. tipsy：醉酒的；喝醉的
3. the Bacchic：酒神节

allowed to drop into the speech of the back streets, or alternatively to spout cloudy inanities[1] in an attempt to rise above vulgarity. Tragedy scorns to babble trivialities, and, like a married woman obliged to dance at a festival, will look rather shamefaced among the wanton satyrs. If ever I write satyric dramas, my dear fellows, I shall not be content to use merely the plain, unadorned language of everyday speech; I shall try not to depart so far from the tone of tragedy as to make no distinction between the speech of a Davus[2], or of a bold-faced Pythias[3] who has managed to trick Simo[4]

---

1. inanities：虚幻
2, 3, 4. Davus, Pythias, Simo：达乌斯、皮提亚斯、西摩都是喜剧中的典型人物。

out of a talent, and that of Silenus[1], who after all was the guardian and attendant of the young god Bacchus. I shall aim at a style that employs no unfamiliar diction, one that any writer might hope to achieve, but would sweat tears of blood in his efforts and still not manage it — such is the power of words that are used in the right places and in the right relationships, and such the grace that they can add to the commonplace when so used. If you are going to bring woodland fauns[2] on to the stage, I do not think you should ever allow them to speak as though they had been brought up in the heart of the city; do not let them be too youthfully indiscreet

---

1. Silenus：森林之神塞利纳斯
2. fauns：半人半羊的农牧之神

in the lines you give them, or crack any filthy or obscene jokes. For such things give offence to those of knightly or freeborn rank and the more substantial citizens; these men do not take kindly to what meets with the approval of the masses, the buyers of roast beans and chestnuts, nor do they give it a prize.

A long syllable following a short one is called an iambus[1], which is a fast-moving foot. From this the name ‘trimeters’ became attached to the iambic line, since it produced six beats; and the metre was the same throughout the line. But not so very long ago, so that it might fall upon the ear with rather more

1. iambus：（诗学中的）抑扬格。如果一个音步中有两个音节，前者为轻，后者为重，则这种音步叫抑扬格音步。

weight and deliberation, the iambic line obligingly opened its ranks to the steady spondee[1], but did not extend its welcome to the point of giving way to it in the second or fourth foot. The true iambic measure is rarely found in the 'noble' trimeters of Accius[2]; and on the verse, too, with which Ennius so ponderously burdened the stage lies the reproach of over-hasty and careless composition, or of ignorance of his art. Not everyone is critical enough to be aware of rhythmical faults in verse, and an indulgence has been shown to our Roman poets that true poets should not need.

---

1. spondee：（诗学中的）扬扬格，一般由连续两个重音节组成。
2. Accius：阿克齐乌斯，古罗马悲剧作家、语言学家。

Is that a reason for loose and lawless writing on my part? Or should I assume that everyone will notice my transgressions, and therefore proceed cautiously, keeping within the bounds in which I may safely hope for indulgence? If I do so, I shall have escaped censure[1], indeed, but shall not have deserved any praise. For yourselves, my friends, you must give your days and nights to the study of Greek models. But, you will say, your grandfathers were enthusiastic about the versification and wit of Plautus. They were altogether too tolerant, not to say foolish, in their admiration of both these things in him, if you and I have any idea of

1. censure：批评

how to discriminate between coarseness[1] and graceful wit, and how to pick out the right rhythm both by counting and by ear.

Thespis[2] is given the credit for having invented tragedy as a new genre; he is said to have taken his plays about to be sung and acted on wagons by players whose faces were smeared with the lees[3] of wine. After him came Aeschylus[4], who devised the mask and the dignified robe of tragedy; it was he who laid down a stage with planks of moderate size, and who introduced

---

1. coarseness：粗鄙
2. Thespis：泰斯庇斯，公元前 6 世纪的古希腊雅典诗人，悲剧的创始者。开创了悲剧中演员和合唱队的对白。
3. lees：酒渣；酒糟
4. Aeschylus：埃斯库罗斯（公元前 525—前 456），古希腊悲剧作家，被誉为“悲剧之父”。

the grand style into tragedy and increased the actor's height with buskins. These playwrights were succeeded by those of the Old Comedy[1], which enjoyed a fairly considerable favour; but its freedom degenerated into an offensive violence of language which had to be curbed by law. This law was observed, and the Chorus, deprived of its right to be abusive, fell into a shamed silence.

Our own poets have tried their hand in every style; and they have enjoyed some of their greatest successes

---

1. the Old Comedy：旧喜剧，公元前 5 世纪左右的古希腊喜剧的初始阶段，通过表演阿里斯劳的作品而闻名。这些剧目大多是政治讽刺剧和社会问题剧，特点是对公众人物和事件进行无情的讽刺和批判。公元前 416 年，雅典颁布了不准针对个人进行讽刺的法律规定，喜剧创作和表演受到约束，遂陷入沉寂。

when they have had the courage to turn aside from the paths laid down by the Greeks and sing of deeds at home, and this in both tragedies and comedies with Roman backgrounds. Indeed Italy would be no less renowned in the arts of language than she is in valour and the arts of war, were it not that her poets, one and all, shrink from the tedious task of polishing their work. But you, my dear fellows, the descendants of Numa Pompilius[1], you must have nothing to do with any poem that has not been trimmed into shape by many a day's toil and much rubbing out, and corrected down to the smallest detail.

---

1. Numa Pompilius：努马·庞皮留斯（公元前 753—前 673），古罗马王政时期第二任国王，皮索家族据说是他的后代。

Because Democritus[1] believes that native genius is worth any amount of piddling art, and will not allow a place on Mount Helicon[2] to poets with rational minds, a good many will not take the trouble to trim their nails and their beards; they haunt solitary places, and keep away from the public baths. For they will gain the repute and title of poets, they think, if they never submit to the ministrations of the barber Licinus a head that all the hellebore of all the Anticyra[3]s in the

1. Democritus：德谟克利特（公元前 460—前 370），古希腊唯物主义哲学家，原子论创始人，政治上属奴隶制民主派，在伦理上认为幸福是人生的目的，真正的幸福在于心神宁静。
2. Mount Helicon：赫里岗，诗神栖居之山，即诗歌领域。
3. Anticyra：安提库拉，是盛产药草的希腊城邦，据说能出产一种治愈神志不清的药（hellebore）。

world could never reduce to sanity. What an ass I am to purge the bile out of my system as the season of spring comes along! Otherwise no man would write better poetry. But the game's not worth the candle. So I will play the part of a whetstone, which can put an edge on a blade, though it is not itself capable of cutting. Even if I write nothing myself, I will teach the poet his duties and obligations; I will tell him where to find his resources, what will nourish and mould his poetic gift, what he may, and may not, do with propriety, where the right course will take him, and where the wrong.

The foundation and fountain-head of good composition is a sound understanding. The Socratic writings will provide you with material, and if you look after the subject-matter the words will come readily enough. The man who has learnt his duty towards his country and his friends, the kind of love he should feel for a parent, a brother, and a guest, the obligations of a senator and of a judge, and the qualities required in a general sent out to lead his armies in the field — such a man will certainly know the qualities that are appropriate to any of his characters. I would lay down that the experienced poet, as an imitative artist, should look to human life and character for his models, and from them derive a language that is true to life. Sometimes a play that has a few brilliant passages showing a true appreciation of character, even if it lacks grace and has little depth or artistry, will catch the fancy of an audience, and keep its attention more firmly than verse which lacks substance but is filled with well-sounding trifles.

To the Greeks the Muses gave native wit and the ability to turn phrases, kind there was nothing they craved more than renown. We Romans in our schooldays learn long calculations for dividing the pound into dozens of parts. 'Here, young Albinus, you tell me: if you take an ounce from five-twelfths of a pound, what's left? Come on now, you could have answered by now.' 'A third of a pound.' 'Good! You'll be able to look after yourself all right. If you add an ounce, what does that come to?' 'A half.' When once this corroding lust for profit has infected our minds, can we hope for poems to be written that are worth rubbing over with cedar oil and storing away in cases of polished cypress?

Poets aim at giving either profit or delight, or at combining the giving of pleasure with some useful precepts for life. When you are giving precepts of any kind, be succinct, so that receptive minds may easily grasp what you are saying and retain it firmly; when the mind has plenty to cope with, anything superfluous merely goes in one ear and out of the other. Works written to give pleasure should be as true to life as possible, and your play should not demand belief for just anything that catches your fancy; you should not let the ogress Lamia gobble up a child, and later bring it out of her belly alive. The centuries of the elder citizens will disapprove of works lacking in edification, while the haughty Ramnes will have nothing to do with plays that are too serious. The man who has managed to blend profit with delight wins everyone's approbation, for he gives his reader pleasure at the same time as he instructs him. This is the book that not only makes money for the booksellers, but is carried to distant lands and ensures a lasting fame for its author.

However, there are faults that we should be ready to forgive; for the lute-string does not always give the note intended by the mind and hand, but often returns a high note when a low one is required, and the bow will not always hit the mark aimed at. When there are plenty of fine passages in a poem, I shall not take exception to occasional blemishes which the poet has carelessly let slip, or which his fallible human nature has not guarded against. What then is our conclusion about this? Just as the literary scribe gets no indulgence if he keeps on making the same mistake however often he is warned, and the lutenist is laughed at if he always goes wrong on the same string, so the poet who is often remiss seems to me another Choerilus[1], whose two or three good lines I greet with

---

1. Choerilus：科利勒斯，古希腊亚历山大时期的三流诗人。

an amused surprise; at the same time I am put out when the worthy Homer nods, although it is natural that slumber should occasionally creep over a long poem.

A poem is like a painting: the closer you stand to this one the more it will impress you, whereas you have to stand a good distance from that one; this one demands a rather dark corner, but that one needs to be seen in full light, and will stand up to the keen-eyed scrutiny of the art-critic; this one only pleased you the first time you saw it, but that one will go on giving pleasure however often it is looked at.

A word to you, the elder of the Piso boys. Though you have been trained by your father to form sound judgements and have natural good sense, take this truth to heart and do not forget it: that only in certain walks of life does the second-rate pass muster. An advocate or barrister of mediocre capacity falls short of the eloquent Messalla[1] in ability, and knows less than Aulus Cascellius, yet he is not without his value; on the other hand, neither gods nor men — nor, for that matter, booksellers — can put up with mediocrity in poets. Just as at a pleasant dinner-party music that is out of tune, a coarse perfume, or poppy-seeds served with bitter Sardinian honey give offence, for the meal could just as well have been given without them, so

1. Messalla：墨萨拉，与贺拉斯同时代的诗人、演说家。

is it with a poem, which is begotten and created for the soul's delight; if it falls short of the top by ever so little, it sinks right down to the bottom. A man who does not understand the games keeps away from the weapons of the Campus Martius, and if he has no skill with the ball or quoit or hoop, he stands quietly aside so that the crowds round the side-lines will not roar with laughter at his expense; yet the man who knows nothing about poetry has the audacity[1] to write it. And why not? he says. He is his own master, a man of good family, and above all he is rated as a knight in wealth and there is nothing against him.

---

1. audacity：勇气

You, I am sure, will not say or do anything counter to the will of Minerva[1]; you have judgement and sense enough for that. But if at any time you do write anything, submit it to the hearing of the critic Maecius, and your father's and mine as well; then put the papers away and keep them for nine years. You can always destroy what you have not published, but once you have let your words go they cannot be taken back.

While men still roamed the forests, they were restrained from bloodshed and a bestial[2] way of life by Orpheus, the sacred prophet and interpreter of

---

1. Minerva：密涅瓦，古罗马神话中的智慧女神。
2. bestial：野蛮的

the divine will — that is why he is said to have tamed tigers and savage lions. Amphion, too, the founder of Thebes, is credited with having moved stones by the strains of his lyre, and led them where he would with this sweet blandishment[1]. At one time this was the way of the wise man: to distinguish between public and personal rights and between things sacred and profane, to discourage indiscriminate sexual union and make rules for married life, to build towns, and to inscribe laws on tablets of wood. For this reason honour and fame were heaped upon the bards, as divinely inspired beings, and upon their songs. After

1. blandishment：引诱；诱惑

them the illustrious Homer and Tyrtaeus[1] fired the hearts of men to martial deeds with their verses. In song, too, oracles were delivered, and the way to right living taught; the favour of kings was sought in Pierian strains[2]; and singing-festivals were devised as a close to the year's long toils. So there is no need for you to blush for the Muse, with her skill in song, and for Apollo the god of singers.

The question has been asked whether a fine poem is the product of nature or of art. I myself cannot see the value of application without a strong natural aptitude,

---

1. Tyrtaeus：提尔泰奥斯，公元前 7 世纪的古希腊哀歌体诗人，第二次美塞尼亚战争期间，他曾用诗歌鼓舞将士战胜敌人。
2. Pierian strains：缪斯女神所弹奏的音乐，这里指代诗歌。

or, on the other hand, of native genius unless it is cultivated — so true is it that each requires the help of the other, and that they enter into a friendly compact with each other. The athlete who strains to reach the winning-post has trained hard as a boy and put up with a great deal, sweating, and shivering in the cold, and keeping away from women and wine; the flautist who plays at the Pythian games[1] has first had to leam his art under a stern master. Yet nowadays it is enough for a man to say: 'I write marvellous poems — the devil take the hindmost! It would be dreadful if I fell behind and had to admit that I know

1. Pythian games：皮托竞技会，是古希腊人为纪念太阳神战胜巨蟒每年举办的全国性的竞技赛会。

absolutely nothing about what, after all, I've never learnt.'

Like the auctioneer[1] who gathers a crowd round him anxious to buy his wares, the poet who has plenty of property and plenty of money accumulating interest is a standing invitation to flatterers to swarm round for what they can make out of him. But if he is a man who can put on a first-class dinner in proper style, or stand security for a poor man of little credit, or rescue him when he is tied up in a dismal lawsuit, I shall be surprised if, for all his apparent happiness, he can tell a true friend from a false. And you, if you have given or intend to give anyone

1. auctioneer：小贩；叫卖者

a present, do not ask him in the first flush of his delight to listen to your own poems. 'Lovely!' he will exclaim. 'That's excellent — it's absolutely first-rate!' He will turn quite pale with emotion, and will even be so amiable as to squeeze out a tear or two; he will dance with excitement, or tap out his approval with his foot. Just as at a funeral the paid mourners are on the whole more active and vocal than those who are really suffering deeply, so the mock admirer shows more appreciation than the man who is sincere in his praise. It is said that when kings are anxious to test thoroughly whether a man is worthy of their friendship, they put him to the trial with wine, and ply[1]

1. ply：通常用作"ply someone with something"，表示"不停地给某人以许多……"。

him with many bumpers. If you are going to write poetry, see to it that you are never put upon by people with the hidden cunning of the fox.

When anything was read to Quintilius Varus, he would say: 'You must put this right — and this too, please.' If after two or three ineffectual attempts you said you could not do any better, he would tell you to get rid of the passage; the lines were badly turned and would have to be hammered out again. If you chose to defend a weakness rather than correct it, he would not say another word, nor waste any effort in trying to prevent you from regarding yourself and your work as unique and unrivalled. An honest, sensible man will condemn any lines that are lifeless, will find fault with them if they are rough, and will run his pen through any that are inelegant; he will cut out any superfluous[1] adornment, will force you to clarify anything that is obscure, and will draw attention to ambiguities; in fact he will prove another Aristarchus[2] and point out everything that requires changing. He will not say, 'Why should I quarrel with a friend over trifles?' Those trifles will bring his friend into serious trouble when once his efforts have been taken amiss and he has become an object of ridicule.

Just as happens when a man is plagued by a nasty

1. superfluous：多余的
2. Aristarchus：阿里斯塔克斯（公元前 217？—前 145？），古希腊语法学家和文献校勘家，亚历山大城图书馆馆长，以校订和研究荷马史诗而闻名。

rash, or by jaundice, or a fit of lunacy[1], so men of sense are afraid to have any dealings with a mad poet, and keep clear of him; but children boldly follow him about and tease him. While he is wandering about, spouting his lines with his head in the air like a fowler[2] intent on his game, he can fall into a well or pit, and no one will bother to pull him out however long he goes on shouting to the passers-by for help. And if anyone should take the trouble to lend a hand and let down a rope, 'How do you know he didn't jump down there on purpose,' I shall say, 'and doesn't want to be rescued?' and I shall tell the story of the Sicilian

---

1. lunacy：精神失常
2. fowler：捕鸟者

poet Empedocles[1]' death. Eager to be regarded as one of the immortal gods, Empedocles in cold blood leapt into the flames of Etna. And poets should have the right to take their own lives. To save a man who does not want to be saved is as good as murdering him. This is not the first time he has tried, and if he is pulled out he will not immediately become a normal human being and abandon his desire to win notoriety by his death. Nor is it very clear why he goes on trying to write poetry — whether because he has defiled his

1. Empedocles：恩培多克勒（公元前 493 或 495—前 432 或 435），古希腊哲学家、诗人、医生，持物活论观点，认为万物皆由火、水、土、气四种元素形成，动力是爱和憎，爱使元素结合，憎使元素分离。

father's ashes, or sacrilegiously[1] violated a place struck by lightning. It is certain, at any rate, that he is raving mad, and like a bear that has been strong enough to burst the bars of its cage, he makes everyone, learned and ignorant alike, take to their heels when he embarks on his detestable recitations. He will fasten on to anyone he manages to catch, and read him to death — just like a leech[2] that will not drop off your skin until it is gorged with blood.

---

1. sacrilegiously：亵渎神明地
2. leech：水蛭

术语汇编与简释

decorum: 合式

妥帖得体。它要求文艺作品在文艺形式、人物性格以及风格方面首尾一致或为有机和谐的整体。

elegiac couplet：挽歌对句

首行六个音步，次行五个音步，最初用于挽歌，后用于赞美歌。

old comedy: 旧喜剧

大多是政治讽刺剧和社会问题剧，公元前416年，雅典制定了不准讽刺个人的法律规定，对喜剧创作产生了很大影响。喜剧很少批评政治，而把重点放在日常生活的现实上。

purple passage: 辞藻过于华丽的文本

原意指“紫色的补丁”，贺拉斯自创，指描述太过夸张或者华丽的句子、段落，有时甚至是整篇文学作品。

Horace

On the Art of Poetry

图书在版编目（CIP）数据

诗艺：导读注释版 = On the Art of Poetry：英文 /（古罗马）贺拉斯著；王厚平，王洁注释. — 上海：上海译文出版社，2021.6

（世界学术经典系列）

书名原文：On the Art of Poetry

ISBN 978-7-5327-8740-1

Ⅰ.①诗… Ⅱ.①贺… ②王… ③王… Ⅲ.①古典诗歌—创作方法—古罗马—英文 Ⅳ.①I546.072

中国版本图书馆 CIP 数据核字（2021）第 073446 号

诗艺（导读注释版）

［古罗马］贺拉斯 著 王厚平 王 洁 导读 注释

责任编辑 / 谭春惠 装帧设计 / 张志全工作室

上海译文出版社有限公司出版、发行

网址：www.yiwen.com.cn

200001 上海福建中路 193 号

江阴市机关印刷服务有限公司印刷

开本 890 × 1240 1/32 印张 3.25 插页 6 字数 29,000

2021 年 6 月第 1 版 2021 年 6 月第 1 次印刷

印数：0,001—3,000 册

ISBN 978-7-5327-8740-1/J · 056

定价：55.00 元

World Academic Classics
世界学术经典·英文版

Marxism
马克思主义

The Communist Manifesto (Marx & Engels)
共产党宣言（马克思、恩格斯）

Chinese Classics
中国经典

论语（汉英对照）
Confucius' Analects

道德经（汉英对照）
Dao De Jing

孟子（汉英对照）
Mencius

庄子（汉英对照）
Zhuangzi

孙子兵法（汉英对照）
Sun Tzu on the Art of War

大学、中庸（汉英对照）
The Way of Learning and The Way to Harmony

Philosophy
哲　学

Republic (Plato)
理想国（柏拉图）

Metaphysics (Aristotle)
形而上学（亚里士多德）

Meditations on First Philosophy (René Descartes)
第一哲学沉思录（笛卡尔）

A Discourse on Method (René Descartes)
方法论（笛卡尔）

Pascal's Pensées (Blaise Pascal)
思想录（帕斯卡尔）

A Treatise of Human Nature (David Hume)
人性论（休谟）

Critique of Pure Reason (Kant)
纯粹理性批判（康德）

Critique of Judgement (Kant)
判断力批判（康德）

The Phenomenology of Mind (Hegel)
精神现象学（黑格尔）

The Logic of Hegel (Hegel)
小逻辑（黑格尔）

The World as Will and Representation (Schopenhauer)
作为意志与表象的世界（叔本华）

Thus Spake Zarathustra (Nietzsche)
查拉图斯特拉如是说（尼采）

Either / Or (Kierkegaard)
非此即彼（克尔凯郭尔）

Ideas: General Introduction to Pure Phenomenology (Husserl)
纯粹现象学导论（胡塞尔）

On First Philosophy (Husserl)
论第一哲学（胡塞尔）

Tractatus Logico-Philosophicus (Wittgenstein)
逻辑哲学论（维特根斯坦）

Philosophical Investigations (Wittgenstein)
哲学研究（维特根斯坦）

Pragmatism (William James)
实用主义（威廉·詹姆斯）

Reconstruction in Philosophy (John Dewey)
哲学的改造（杜威）

Time and Free Will (Henri Bergson)
时间与自由意志（伯格森）

A Discourse on the Positive Spirit (Auguste Comte)
论实证精神（孔德）

Novum Organum (Francis Bacon)
新工具（培根）

Ethics
伦理学

The Nicomachean Ethics of Aristotle (Aristotle)
尼各马可伦理学（亚里士多德）

The Theory of Moral Sentiments (Adam Smith)
道德情操论（亚当·斯密）

A Discourse on Inequality (Rousseau)
论人类不平等的起源与基础（卢梭）

Critique of Practical Reason (Kant)
实践理性批判（康德）

Utilitarianism (Mill)
功利主义（密尔）

Principia Ethica (Moore)
伦理学原理（摩尔）

Religion
宗教学

Confessions (St. Augustine)
忏悔录（圣·奥古斯丁）

Basic Writings of Saint Thomas Aquinas (St. Thomas Aquinas)
圣托马斯·阿奎那基本著作（阿奎那）

Basic Theological Writings (Martin Luther)
路德基本著作选（马丁·路德）

The Courage to Be (Paul Tillich)
存在的勇气（蒂利希）

The Essence of Christianity (Ludwig Feuerbach)
基督教的本质（费尔巴哈）

Politics
政治学

The Politics of Aristotle (Aristotle)
政治学（亚里士多德）

The Prince (Machiavelli)
君主论（马基雅维利）

The Social Contract (Rousseau)
社会契约论（卢梭）

Leviathan (Thomas Hobbes)
利维坦（霍布斯）

Two Treatises of Government (John Locke)
政府论（洛克）

The Spirit of the Laws (Montesquieu)
论法的精神（孟德斯鸠）

Democracy in America (Tocqueville)
论美国民主（托克维尔）

Considerations on Representative Government (Mill)
代议制政府（密尔）

The Federalist Papers (Hamilton)
联邦党人文集（汉密尔顿）

The Ancien Régime and the Revolution (Tocqueville)
旧制度与大革命（托克维尔）

Utopia (Thomas More)
乌托邦（莫尔）

On Liberty (Mill)
论自由（密尔）

Reflections on the Revolution in France (Edmund Burke)
法国革命论（伯克）

The Will to Power (Nietzsche)
权力意志（尼采）

On War (Carl von Clausewitz)
战争论（克劳塞维茨）

Mutual Aid: A Factor of Evolution (Pyotr Alexeyevich Kropotkin)
互助论（克鲁泡特金）

Economics
经济学

The Economics of Welfare (Pigou)
福利经济学（庇古）

Principles of Economics (Alfred Marshall)
经济学原理（马歇尔）

The General Theory of Employment, Interest and Money (Keynes)
就业、利息与货币通论（凯恩斯）

The Theory of Economic Development (Schumpeter)
经济发展理论（熊彼特）

An Inquiry into the Nature and Causes of the Wealth of Nations (Adam Smith)
国民财富的性质和原因的研究（亚当·斯密）

Capitalism, Socialism and Democracy (Schumpeter)
资本主义、社会主义与民主（熊彼德）

An Essay on Population (Thomas Robert Malthus)
人口原理（马尔萨斯）

The Principles of Scientific Management (Frederick Winslow Taylor)
科学管理原理（泰勒）

Sociology
社会学

Suicide: A Study in Sociology (Durkheim)
自杀：社会学研究（迪尔凯姆）

The Protestant Ethic and the Spirit of Capitalism (Max Weber)
新教伦理与资本主义精神（韦伯）

The Philosophy of Money (George Simmel)
货币哲学（西美尔）

A Treatise on General Sociology (Vilfredo Pareto)
社会学总论（帕累托）

Ideology and Utopia (Mannheim)
意识形态与乌托邦（曼海姆）

First Principles (Herbert Spencer)
基本原理（斯宾塞）

The Theory of Leisure Class (Thorstein B. Veblen)
论闲逸阶级（凡勃伦）

Anthropology
人类学

The Golden Bough (Frazer)
金枝（弗雷泽）

Argonauts of the Western Pacific (Malinowski)
西太平洋的航海者（马林诺夫斯基）

Structure and Function in Primitive Society (Redcliffe-Brown)
原始社会的结构和功能（拉迪克里夫-布朗）

Race, Language and Culture (Franz Boas)
种族·语言·文化（鲍斯）

The Savage Mind (Claude Lévi-Strauss)
野性思维（列维-斯特劳斯）

Psychology
心理学

The Principles of Psychology (William James)
心理学原理（威廉·詹姆斯）

Principles of Physiological Psychology (Wundt)
生理心理学原理（冯特）

The Interpretation of Dreams (Sigmund Freud)
梦的解析（弗洛伊德）

The Archetypes and the Collective Unconscious (Jung)
原型与集体无意识（荣格）

Law
法　学

Ancient Law (Maine)
古代法（梅因）

English Law and the Renaissance (Maitland)
英国法律与文艺复兴（梅特兰）

Lectures on Jurisprudence (Austin)
法理学演讲录（奥斯丁）

Fundamental Principles of the Sociology of Law (Ehrlich)
法律社会学基本原理（埃利希）

History
历史学

The Histories (Herodotus)
历史（希罗多德）

The Peloponnesian War (Thucydides)
伯罗奔尼撒战争史（修昔底德）

The Annals of Imperial Rome (Tacitus)
编年史（塔西佗）

The City of God (St. Augustine)
上帝之城（圣·奥古斯丁）

On Heroes, Hero Worship, and the Heroic in History (Thomas Carlyle)
论历史上的英雄、英雄崇拜和英雄业绩（卡莱尔）

The Idea of History (Collingwood)
历史的观念（科林伍德）

History of Civilization in Europe (Francois Guizot)
欧洲文明史（基佐）

The Influence of Sea Power (Alfred T. Mahan)
海权对历史的影响（马汉）

Theory & History of Historiography (Benedetto Croce)
史学理论与史学史（克罗齐）

A Short Account of the Destruction of the Indies (Bartolomé de las Cases)
西印度毁灭述略（卡萨斯）

Literary Theory and Aesthetics
文学理论与美学

On the Art of Poetry (Aristotle)
诗学（亚里士多德）

On the Art of Poetry (Horace)
诗艺（贺拉斯）

On the Sublime (Longinus)
论崇高（朗吉努斯）

Theory of Aesthetic / History of Aesthetic (Benedetto Croce)
美学理论 / 美学史（克罗齐）

Hegel's Aesthetics Lectures on Fine Art (Hegel)
黑格尔美学讲演录（黑格尔）

The Birth of Tragedy (Nietzsche)
悲剧的诞生（尼采）

Linguistics
语言学

Course in General Linguistics (Saussure)
普通语言学教程（索绪尔）

On Language (Humboldt)
论语言（威廉·洪堡特）

Scientific Philosophy
自然科学哲学

On the Origin of Species (Charles Darwin)
物种起源（达尔文）

Mathematical Principles of Natural Philosophy and Its System of the World (Issac Newton)
自然哲学及其宇宙体系的数学原理（牛顿）

Natural History (Pliny the Elder)
自然史（老普林尼）